CW00762249

Dark Tunnel

of Grace

Dark Tunnel
of Grace

Nadia Serroukh

Copyright © 2024 Nadia Serroukh

The moral right of the author has been asserted.

Apart from any fair dealing for the purposes of research or private study,
or criticism or review, as permitted under the Copyright, Designs and Patents
Act 1988, this publication may only be reproduced, stored or transmitted, in
any form or by any means, with the prior permission in writing of the
publishers, or in the case of reprographic reproduction in accordance with
the terms of licences issued by the Copyright Licensing Agency. Enquiries
concerning reproduction outside those terms should be sent to the publishers.

Troubador Publishing Ltd
Unit E2 Airfield Business Park,
Harrison Road, Market Harborough,
Leicestershire. LE16 7UL
Tel: 0116 2792299
Email: books@troubador.co.uk
Web: www.troubador.co.uk

ISBN 978 1836281 429

British Library Cataloguing in Publication Data.
A catalogue record for this book is available from the British Library.

Printed and bound by CPI Group (UK) Ltd, Croydon, CR0 4YY
Typeset in 11pt Minion Pro by Troubador Publishing Ltd, Leicester, UK

A woman, a stainless soul; character simple, yet misunderstood. Her hair long and dark. Her face oval and kind, eyes that glitter with sorrow and pain. A smile that heals the world and a laughter that enthrals your soul. Her heart is gentle and of pure gold. Her conduct of elegance and grace, the self-sufficient kind you'd want by your side. Her nature is fierce; her judgment is firm. Her words are often harsh yet necessary in life. She stands tall and proud, with conviction in her every stride. Present but with a distant look in her eyes.

From a distance, the world can't see beyond her smile, beauty and elegance. She doesn't give much away, and she is unaware of the power that it creates, a mirage in the desert. If you find yourself close to her, listening intently is when you'll hear her whispers of words that open to bear her heart to the world. The wall she built around herself will always stand it's part of her. She appears in your life in a timely way to lend a hand, sometimes to help you understand your pain.

Her mysterious soul taps into the spiritual world as though her umbilical cord was left uncut. Her words feel like a message exclusively for your heart and soul. She often says, "all things are preordained"; perhaps this helps reaffirm her courage and grace in a world not so kind. She feels disconnected from the world. Unchanged from the child she was.

Looking out at the city view and up at the sky of navy blue. The stars will soon appear; they gather every night and glow. I wonder if they have sorrows of their own. Within my sight, yet beyond my reach. The mysteries of what we don't know. I stand up from the chair and walk towards the glass wall, a perfect window from ceiling to floor, allowing for the perfect view. Skyscrapers and the lights on some levels. The city at my door. Fewer people walking than the hour before.

Life has many veils; we were always under the same one until fate took you away. Living with your ghost, I'm struggling to survive, losing you has placed me in a maze. There comes a time in everyone's life when they'll feel they've been wronged in some way, and things just stopped working. For me, that time has come too soon. A sister who is no longer here, parents I lost to grief, people who have wronged me, and a career which has just begun.

I lean my body against the glass wall and contemplate life. At some point everyone I knew was happy and living life to the full. Today, we are all in a burdened state and desperate for an escape. Responsibility: although its purpose is often difficult to shoulder, bear it we must. It will see us fall and separated from our desires. What nobler cause could we have than to brace against our purpose, to uphold the hand we were dealt, with poise?

These responsibilities will place you on a stage, to be blamed for your failures, and the failures of others. There are only two paths that can be taken. Your burdens will strengthen you and glorify you, or they will lead you down a tunnel that will narrow in time. Your mind, if you can fight it, will be your saviour.

Looking down at my watch, I see it's 9pm. Maybe I'll leave work for another day; the past always brings me down.

"Anyone still here?" the security guard shouts out, distracting my thoughts.

"Yes, I'm here, I'll be working late tonight," I shout back.

"OK, miss, anyone else left on your floor, or just you?"

"Just me."

"OK, this is just a security check, if you need anything please let me know; I'm here till 6am – that's when my shift ends."

"I know, Mikal, thank you."

As he walks away, I look back at the sky and find her to be a darker shade of blue. I wonder if she's OK with the world seeing her in this dark state, emotions on display. Maybe it's OK living with an open heart, when at a distance. I know when I'm in a dark place I remain at a distance and wear a smile to conceal my pain.

I stood here the same time last week and thought about all those many people in my life. The ones who played their games, and the ones who didn't. I still think about them sometimes. The sky grounds me, when I look up at it, it allows me to address each moment, each feeling and each thought. Life is just memories, and I'd do well to remember that there is much I don't remember.

I believe a day will come when all shall see the consequences of their deeds. Life has become a stage for complaints, full of anger, sadness, and rage. When did we get here? Turning on each other day by day. Who has whispered in our ears? Who has planted seeds in our minds? Let us come back and reconsider our ways. Starting with mutual respect. We must drop the who's right and wrong and know there is a place for us all.

I'm contemplating whether I should do a little more work or just sit here and reflect and listen to my inner voice. Reflecting on the past always makes me feel unwell. Melancholy runs deep in my veins. I'm starting to feel a deepening desire to write; it's easier than talking. Not that I have anyone to talk to.

A dark shadow takes over my heart. I feel now that I don't want to remember how much of me I gave, to no avail. It deepens my pain. Before she passed, she would sit and listen to me talk when the heart became burdened. Her last words were:

My entire life I have known you, and I have cherished those fleeting moments of companionship. The depth of your despair, the yearnful mourning of your absent gaze, I could see it and I have tried to comfort you where I could, but I regret my inability to tend to your grief. Time has crept ever on, and in its march, it had not been kind to you. Now I see you can bear it no more. I'm here now, and I pray you speak to me of that which burdens you. Tell me of what has changed and the stories that changed them. Seize this night as your own and bear your pain to me again. From dusk till dawn, I will not speak. I will listen.

Comforted by the memory of these words, I feel a warm breeze, and know that she is here with me again; to listen? So, I take a deep breath to help me open my heart and release my thoughts. I will seize this night and I hope to lighten my sorrows; I know that this will help me survive to the break of dawn. I'll lift my pen and write down my pain.

Every couple of years my heart would overflow with sorrow; if you were here, I know what you would say, because you've said it many times before. "You did not create the world, so you'll never understand it. Focus on what you can create." I miss you.

It has been two years since God called your name. Your car crashed and the doctors were late. The day we were told you weren't coming home, and we would have to prepare your body for your grave, grief consumed us entirely; we were lowered into the ground with you that day. Mother fell to her knees and screamed your name. "Lord, give her back; it's not too late; I can't accept this fate." She thought if she kept asking, something would change. Women gathered around her with tears racing down their faces; "Have faith," they cried out, holding her tight, "the dead cannot bear your lamentations; rejoice for her sake; she is in her resting place." Family, friends and many I did not know prayed for you. They knew you'd gone to a better place; they seemed sure of it.

Father held his gaze, his eyes fixed at the sky as though seeing your soul ascend away. Others stood around your grave with strength shrouding their face; it was a splendid masquerade. When your coffin touched the ground, the angels held your soul, ready to take you home. Your departure; a great story of its own.

You can't take anything with you, I'm told, except three things: the blessings of ongoing charity, beneficial knowledge and the prayers of people who will remember you. You have taken all these with you, and I believe more.

I put the pen down and wipe a tear from my eyes. Life, I'm sure, will never be the same. Prayer and patience, right? I don't know how the system is designed, but I wonder if God really needed to take her? I wish I could understand; that, at least, would be a step in the direction of healing. I take a deep breath and lift my pen and continue writing.

Do you remember the days when love, joy and laughter dictated our ways? How did I get to anger, sorrow and rage? I can't seem to remember. I am in a dark tunnel and can't seem to find my way to God's grace. My heart often asks the two angels, are you fighting to take me away? The angel of death luring me to the grave, the angel of life pulling me away.

We grew up together and we were inseparable. Family, I thought, were supposed to stand together. Whoever needed help always called for me. Whoever needed empathy came to cry their tears to me. Healing they found in me. Where was mine in them? Except you.

The fun, the laughter and tears we shared are nothing but a ghost in my ears. Where had I gone wrong? I beg to hear. Have they deceived my loving heart, or is it I who deceived myself? Desperate for love all my life. The mother I never had, compensating for that love, I opened myself to a pain greater than my gain. The child I never was, the games I never played. The love I never felt. I have fooled myself with the idea of a together, and a forever. A hopeless romantic, a fool in life and a fool in love.

My home was an open door. My loving heart created love and joy. The music and the food, the chatter, and the laughter. Oh, how much love we had, I thought. They always came running to my home; how sweet is love when it's yours. Reality showed me I was nothing but a fool. They reduced me to a clown to entertain them with laughter and free food. The scales of justice will weigh our deeds.

If you should ever want to know in whose hearts you reside, ask someone to do something for you, and that will be the day the truth unveils. My pain often pleads, may God strike them down! They have played my gentle loving heart. But the love in me hopes for another way.

Am I wrong in what I say or what I feel? Is my anger, sadness and rage misplaced? Did my pain find its aim, or was it a mask that had shrouded my eyes?

I had been deceived. I realise now my reality was their stage. I don't know who's right and wrong, but I think that is a question for judgement day. All I know is that the scales of justice do not lie. Let me tell you something else – I hoped that one day my troubles could end. I had a dream that showed me this will remain a hope and nothing more. I live in despair, wondering why I must never find a way out of this dark tunnel I'm in. I can't seem to see the light. I just hope that God can shine his grace.

I remember going away for a few days, hoping that I could find a reason to feel OK. I sat on a bench; soon after, a young boy about the age of five or six was made to dance, collecting his money at the end. He looked at me and smiled. I felt a whisper from his heart: the child I never was, the games I never played, the love I never felt. He continued to walk by. I smiled back at him with tears in my eyes, giving him a piece of my heart. I am with you in pain, oh son of mine.

I went out to lighten the burden in my heart; I came back with one greater than I could bear. Is this my fate, oh Lord? Where is your mercy? Have you seen my dying heart? I beg you claim me back! In me, there is nothing left.

I have devoted my life to those I love; living in fear, and yet hope, that they'd catch a glimpse of my despair. I hide behind the laughter and the smile. How can it be that, till this day, not one of them feels my pain? In me they see nothing more than comfort, laughter and gain. When did I get here? I can't remember the day.

That young boy now lives in my mind; I often think of him to survive; perhaps in that fleeting moment, he found a mother in me. I find myself *whispering, "I love you, my son." I think I find comfort when I see that struggle is all around.*

Tell me, what am I to do? Shall I stop here, or continue? Dawn is yet to rise, though I am feeling tired and need the sleep. I fear the next time we meet, I might be six foot deep.

Every time I try to take my life, the Arab proverb prevails: "if you want to die, throw yourself in the ocean. You'll find yourself fighting to survive. You don't want to kill yourself. You want to kill something inside of you, something that burdens your soul". This I find to be truer than my heart would admit. Am I willing to survive?

Looking at my watch again, although it's almost 11pm, I feel the desire to carry on writing. The night will soon end; hopefully my heart can find a little space to carry on.

Maybe there is good yet to come. Until then, I am in a desperate state. Abandoned without a glimpse of hope to light my path. Is it true what they say, Lord, that you exist everywhere? Can I catch a glimpse of your grace? I think you built the world in six days; on the seventh you said, "Let there be light."

Did you forget me in the dark?

I remember a dream I often have:

*I walk into a house which is mine, but not as it is in
waking life.*
It is huge and beautifully decorated.
Floors of marble and mosaic walls.
Chandeliers emanating a bright light.
*Every room I enter leads me to another room
greater in size and beauty.*
In awe of what I see, I smile and say to myself:
"Surely this can't be mine?"
I continue to walk through each room,
*and each room continues to lead me into another
room greater in size.*
Endless space, each room with its own unique feature.
*One of the rooms has steps, which lead me to
another part of the house I did not know existed.*
*Huge mahogany double doors in front of my face. I
push them open with ease and find an amazing space.*
*I start to wonder and plan, what would I do with
all this glorious space?*
I shout out and say:
"My Lord, are my days yet to come?"

When I wake up, it is with a renewed soul. I'm not
sure what the dream means, but it makes me feel
good, so here's to another day.

Distracting my mind from my thoughts, I look at my blank computer for a moment; the soft glow of a black screen comforts me. Then, returning to the memory of that darkness that covered my heart a couple of hours ago, suddenly my heart is pierced by an ember of light. I feel hope run through my heart and my spirit is revived. I lay my hand on the window. *I love how it's from ceiling to floor.* I smile up at the sky. Is it in darkness you contemplate, plan, and create life? Pain is never in vain. To this beautiful sky, I speak a whisper from my heart:

Dear sky, in this dark tunnel I call your name; you hold the spirit of my sister. Please tell her that I can hear her words in my heart; to feel her spirit is alive is enough for me to survive. I know we will meet again, but not yet.

I found you in my dream. In awe of what I saw, I froze before your gate. Your palace made of rubies and corals, marble floors and mosaic walls. Chandeliers dripping with diamonds and pearls. Your tent, a hollow pearl sixty miles wide. Rivers of wine; streams of milk and honey before your feet. Surrounded by gardens of eternity and cedar trees, a kingdom for your soul. What a magnificent home; your perpetual residence. You recline upon your throne, adorned with bracelets of gold. Draped in green, a garment of fine silk, embroidered in gold. Your eyes lined with kohl. Your scent of white musk lingers in the air. Peace lights your face. Your spirit is unchanged, full of beauty and grace. You have found your resting place. May peace be your eternal reign. I no longer question my pain. Life is never in vain. I now understand death. To God we belong; to God we shall return.

Time heals. I have found strength to deal with fate. This spider's web irritates me, the Norns pester us and play with us, and mock us. Sometimes I curse them too.

I went to see Mum and Dad last week. They still ask about you. I hate that they can't remember; I hate that I'm the only one of us left that remembers you're gone. I can't blame them; I can't blame them for being sick. I always knew their dementia was going to be hard on us. I know I was scared; I didn't want them to forget us. But they still remember me; they still remember you.

They don't remember that you're not here anymore, and I can't bear having to be the one to tell them again and again that you're not here anymore. So, I stopped telling them. I know it's selfish; I know it's not fair that I don't tell them.

Even if they forget, they deserve to know every time, that you're not with us anymore.

I know that I should tell them again and again that there was a crash, that you didn't make it. I can't keep watching their eyes when they realise; I can't keep hearing her scream when I tell her, just to have to do it again the following week.

I think I hate even more that sometimes they call me by your name; and that I play along with it. I hate that sometimes I blame you for leaving me, and that I have to do it alone.

Family and friends don't come and visit anymore. It's clear now, that we were only great to them when they were hosting a stage of free food and laughter. Life becomes a lonely place the day you realise how many people were only around for what you gave them.

I've been lost for two years, since you left us. My sister and my friend. When we buried you, darkness enveloped my heart and soul, sending me trudging into this dark tunnel, but I've found God's light. It is faint and far, and yet I see that it shines brightly and honestly, and I cherish what little sight it gives me in this blackness. It gives me a way out. I have seen your resting place in this light. It fills me with joy and renews in me a desire to live, and I know that I will see you again one day, but not yet.

Destiny: I believe it means power; to me at least. Every word you utter holds power. I remember when I was eight years old, and you were ten years old, and you said, "I want to be your John the Baptist; I believe in you." I didn't know what you meant at the time, but after you passed, I realised what you were trying to say. John believed his purpose in life was to make way for the Messiah and that when he is sure that he is the one, he will fall so that the Messiah may rise. You didn't have love for the world, only me and our parents. We didn't need friends because we had each other, and I thought it would always stay like that. Maybe we speak destiny into our lives; maybe we can think it into reality. Controlled and focused thought and energy. Maybe if I can bend my entire will; my energy, into thinking and feeling just one thing, maybe I'll see it more clearly, and maybe it'll see me.

Looking back at my watch, it's 1am; I think I'm tired. Reflecting and writing tonight has served me well. I should book a taxi home; hopefully I can get a few hours' sleep before starting another day's work. The sky is black now; I feel it's time to go home.

I switch off my computer, unplug my laptop and put it in my bag. My coat on my arm. Heading to the lifts, the doors open just as I arrive. An older man greets me with a smile.

"To the ground floor?" he asks.

"Please," I reply and enter.

Leaning back on the lift wall, I notice that he is strangely perfect. Not in the vain sense where every detail is tended to, but in the perfectly imperfect way. His shirt is wrinkled and his beard overgrown, but the crease line on his shirt is the straightest I have ever seen, and although his beard is overgrown, it complements his complexion. His skin glows with an olive tan, and the lines on his face appear to centre at his eyes, which gaze down onto the resin floor, scuffed by its occupants over time.

His eyes are kind, and it's clear he has been working all night as his eyes have grown red with tiredness.

As the lift doors open, he looks at me and gestures with his hand.

"After you," he says with a soft smile.

Exiting the lift, I look over at Mikal.

"Thank you, goodnight," I say as he holds the revolving door to stop it from swinging, allowing me a way out, where I'm met by cold air.

I look up at the sky and send a whisper from my heart: *I won't see you tomorrow as I'll be home, which does not have a window from ceiling to floor; my walls are made of brick and the windows are small. I have much more to say, so I'll look up at you soon.* As I get into a taxi, I feel relief. At the end of a dark tunnel, you'll find God's grace.

Despair is a well – you can look down and never see the water at the bottom and there will be nothing but darkness. If you gaze for too long, if you allow the tunnel to draw you in and consume you, you will fall and drown in your own mind. Look to the bottom regardless, and labour to draw the bucket up. And you will see that there is water, and it will be clear and clean. Only then will you understand this dark tunnel, and what it holds. I have gazed into this well long enough; this melancholy is real. But surely, I must also realise that it is blinding; there is more that I have not seen that will guide me out.

I wake up the next morning at home; the light comes through the window, drawing my eyes to the sky; it never looks the same, ever evolving. I was told there are ninety-nine doors in life – for one to open, another must close. Each door being a pathway to experience something new; sorrow, anger and rage are doors I have closed now, but what about grief? Am I ready for that to close? Life is never going to wait; it is orbiting two doors – birth and return – haven't I once caught a glimpse of God's grace? Perhaps I only walked past that door but was caught by grief. Like the stars that light the sky, I want my life to light the world with love, laughter and joy.

Emotions have profound meaning in and of themselves, but what is light in the absence of darkness, heaven in the absence of hell, or the sky in the absence of the ground? One gives meaning to the other. No experience, no emotion, is lesser, nor greater, than the next; they are all equal. Should the heart choose to live fully, it must search for them all. I had been stuck at the doors of anger, sorrow and rage for too long, only to then arrive at loss and grief. I want to experience all that I can and must endure the hand of fate with poise and humility. I have done the best I can, but today I know I must do better than I have; close these doors, which have brought nothing but pain. Perhaps the hand of fate can redirect my course to love, laughter and joy.

Emotions are a maze.
Have hope and you will find your way.
Destiny is working to direct
your course.

Dear Sephra,

I've missed you so much.

After I spoke to you that night, I felt such a huge relief, like I knew that I was going to be OK. I didn't know how and I didn't know when or why, but I felt like this veil had been taken off my face and I could see a little bit clearer, a little bit further, and I could think more freely.

When there's so much going on in your mind and there's no one to speak to, it all becomes a little bit fuzzy and jumbled. When I speak to you, it makes everything a little simpler.

It felt like putting everything down on a table so that I could see what I had in my pockets.

I realised that writing my thoughts and feelings down in a letter to you was healing. I will continue for as long as I feel I need to, and I think you'll be glad to hear from me again, but I promise I won't be so depressive.

We had family over last week. Technically they invited themselves over, but they brought everything with them: Freya brought her lasagne and Millie brought that salad thing she makes with the little bread pieces. I opened the door, thinking to myself, *what on earth is going on?* but I couldn't refuse them, could I?

I have to admit, as much as I don't want to, that I enjoyed it. We sat in the conservatory, and I sat in my normal seat next to the door. I'd missed them, and there were some new faces too. Freya has a little girl, and she really is something special.

It was a heart-warming evening, full of laughter and joy, and it all seemed like nothing had changed. I wish you were there with us, but I'm sure you were. I remember thinking, to what extent do our emotions deceive us and turn us against each other?

I've got an early morning tomorrow; I joined a running club.

I'll write to you soon.

Love you.

Dear Sephra,

I looked in the mirror and realised I didn't like what I saw.

So, I bought a membership again. Robert told me last time that if I stopped, I'd realise very quickly what all that work was really for, and he wasn't wrong. So, I'm really going to try and fix myself up. Talking, well… writing, clears my mind and helps me focus on everything else that needs my focus.

I went to the gym this morning and it felt amazing.

I'm slowly putting my life back together again. Obviously, I still have moments here and there, but I know it takes time and that's normal. But slowly, right?

I've stopped trying to live life on my terms, and I've started living life on life's terms.

I'll write to you soon.

Dear Sephra,

Work is going well, very busy but it's good. The usual world of finance, month end, quarter end, year end, it always comes round so fast. Process for this, and process for that. Why don't we start writing process notes on writing a process note, and then maybe they'll ask me what my process was for writing my process note.

I think at this point, I just want them to process my middle finger too.

Meeting about this, and meeting about that. It never ends. But I really do enjoy it.

I am feeling better with each letter I write, so, I'll write to you soon.

Dear Sephra,

It's funny looking back at all the things I wrote that night in the office. I was in a dark place, and I still am in some way.

I just had so much to say, and no order to tell it in. It helps to talk, but when you have no one to talk to, writing works just as well.

My heart is now experiencing a perfect stillness; I feel present in almost everything I do.

I'll write to you soon.

Love you.

Dear Sephra,

Dad passed away.

Dear Sephra,

We all knew it was going to happen sooner or later, and I've been coming to terms with it for a while now. I think I accepted it before it even happened. I feel guilty that it hasn't affected me as much as yours did. Is that fair?

I miss him too now, but I accepted it a long time ago, and at this point I think I'm happy he's comfortable now, in that little cottage he always dreamt of.

Say hi to him for me.

Dear Sephra,

I don't remember when I last wrote; I can't find my diary, so I've opened a new one.

I met someone… you would love this man; he is great, handsome too, he is kind and caring and works hard. He's very grounded too.

I'll write to you soon.

Dear Sephra,

It's been a while, I've been busy, but I've not forgotten you.

Many positive things are finally happening; life has decided that it's my turn.

After so much heartache, I can finally know what it's like to live.

I'll write soon. I'm not sure how soon though.

PS We decided to call her Meriam.

Dear Sephra,

We have welcomed into our lives another new
arrival, and the days are getting busier.

I'm happy.

I'll write to you soon.

PS We called him Isaac.

Dear Sephra,

I went back to our café. I took Meriam with me, and she went straight to your chair. I'm writing this letter from here now.

I just wanted you to know.

Love you.

Emotions have a profound meaning in and of themselves,
but what is light in the absence of darkness,
heaven in the absence of hell,
or the sky in the absence of the ground?
One gives meaning to the other.
No experience, no emotion, is lesser, nor greater,
than the next; they are all equal.
Should the heart choose to live fully,
it must search for them all.

I.Z

Never give up on yourself.
Tough times will come and test you.
Good times will crown you,
but the cycle will never stop.
Life has a duty to refine you.
Be relentless.
Be steadfast.
Your time will come.
Believe it with conviction.

May peace be your eternal reign.